The Case of the Missing Trophy

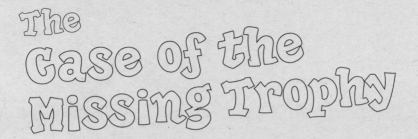

The Case of the Missing Trophy

Angela Shelf Medearis

Illustrated by Robert Papp

SCHOLASTIC INC.

New York   Toronto   London   Auckland   Sydney
Mexico City   New Delhi   Hong Kong   Buenos Aires

ISBN 0-439-52325-7

Text copyright © 2004 by Angela Shelf Medearis.
Illustrations copyright © 2004 by Scholastic Inc.

12 11 10   14 15 16/0

Printed in the U.S.A.   40

First printing, October 2004

Contents

1
Decisions, Decisions!

Cameron Thompson's heart raced. He wiped his sweaty palms on his jacket even though there was frost on the trees outside. "Mom, can you let me out here, please?"

"I don't mind driving you to the front of the school. We're a good three blocks away."

"I need the exercise, Mom," Cameron said. "Everybody says kids don't get enough exercise anymore."

"You get plenty of exercise, Cameron," Pat Thompson said, smiling. "What's this *really* about? Did you forget your homework?"

"No, Mom. I just want to walk," Cameron said with a shrug. He hoped this made it sound like he didn't really care one way or the other. "No big deal. Dad always lets me out here."

Why had he said that? His mother didn't like it when he compared her to his dad. She'd been like that ever since they got divorced a few years ago. Now she'd never let him walk the rest of the way.

Cameron sighed heavily as they pulled up in front of Pecan Springs Elementary School. After his parents' divorce, Cameron's mom had moved to Houston, Texas. Cameron visited his mother every other weekend, during the summers, and on holidays. A few weeks ago, his mother decided to move back to Austin, Texas. Her new house was only a few blocks away from where Cameron lived with his dad.

Cameron was happy his mom was back in town. But he didn't like the way she always wanted to kiss and hug him like she did when he was little.

Cameron stared out the car window. There was no doubt this would be the longest walk of his nine-year-old life. If he could just hop out and race into the school, everything would be fine. But Cameron knew his mother — there was no chance that was going to happen.

The car sat in front of the school. "Cameron, are you getting out? What's the matter?" his mom asked. "Don't want to leave me, huh? I understand. Don't worry. I'll pick you up right after school. Now that I'm here in Austin, we're going to spend a lot of time together. Your dad will have you one week and then you'll be with me for a week. That's a lot better than just seeing you on holidays, every other weekend, and during the summer, isn't it? Now give me a kiss good-bye."

The last thing Cameron wanted to do was hurt his mother's feelings, but Miguel and Jessie, his two best friends, were watching him from the school's steel double doors. If they saw Cameron's mother treating him like a baby, they would tease him. Cameron had to tell her the truth. He gulped loudly. It felt like he had a lump as big as a baseball in his throat.

"Cameron," his mom said, "are you going with me to work, or what?"

"No, Mom. It's just that, well, I don't want to make a big deal about saying good-bye," Cameron said. He didn't dare look at his mom. She was probably crying by now. His dad was cool with Cameron growing up. But his mom wanted him to stay her "little baby" forever.

"You mean you don't want a hug and a kiss?" she asked.

"Later, Mom," Cameron said, still staring out the window. "You know, inside the house or something."

"Okay," his mother said. "I understand. From now on, we'll just shake hands when I drop you off at school."

Cameron whipped his head around. His mother wasn't crying!

"Come on. Shake my hand and get going.

4

I don't want to be late for work. Here," she said, grabbing his hand and shaking it vigorously. "You have a nice day, Mr. Cameron."

"'Bye, Mom," Cameron said as he got out of the car. Cameron smiled. He had been afraid all morning that his mother would grab him in front of everyone, give him a huge bear hug, and plant a big kiss on his forehead. She usually did that, even if he asked her not to. What was going on? Maybe his dad told her how it embarrassed him. Cameron was just glad his mother understood.

As soon as Cameron pushed open the doors to the school, he heard, "Hey, Cam, you taking pictures today?"

It was Oscar, Miguel's big brother. He was making fun of Cameron's name, as usual. Lately he'd been calling him "Camera." Now he loomed over Cameron like a giant.

Miguel ran over, and Jessie followed him. "Leave him alone, Oscar, or I'll tell Mom," Miguel said.

Cameron smiled. No matter how big and bad Oscar pretended to be, the mention of his mother set him straight every time.

"Hey, it was just a joke," Oscar said. Then he walked away.

"Thanks, Miguel," Cameron said.

"No problem," Miguel said. "He knows my mother doesn't like him teasing us. Did you do your homework?"

"Yeah, I'm ready," Jessie said.

"Me, too," Cameron said.

"Well, that's a change," Tarann said as she passed by the boys. Tarann was the smartest girl in the class, and one of Cameron's best friends. "I'm glad you're finally learning how to do homework, Cameron. We'd better go in before the last bell rings."

Cameron opened his backpack. He saw his math book, but his English book wasn't there.

"Oh, no, I forgot my English book!" he said.

Then he remembered that his book was

sitting on the desk in his bedroom. The only problem was, it was on the desk at his father's house. He'd forgotten to pack it on Sunday when he left to spend this week at his mother's house. Cameron was always forgetting something.

"What's the problem?" Miguel asked. "Why are you standing there? We'll be late for class."

Cameron said, "I left my English book at my dad's house."

"Not again!" Jessie said. "Every week, you leave something you need at the wrong house."

"And my homework was in my book," Cameron said.

"Oh, no," Miguel said. "We have our English lesson first."

"Mrs. Nunn is not going to be happy," Cameron said as the bell rang.

Sometimes Cameron liked having all three of his best friends in his class. But on the other hand, it made it even more embarrassing when he was in trouble for forgetting something. Cameron could already tell that today was going to be one of those days.

Mrs. Nunn stood at the chalkboard. "I have a wonderful surprise," she said.

"What is it?" everyone seemed to ask at once.

"It's about the Science Fair and the first-place trophy," Mrs. Nunn said with a smile.

Cameron sat up. He stopped by the awards case in the front hall of the school every day so he could look at the Science Fair trophy. It was one of the biggest trophies he'd ever seen.

"As you know," Mrs. Nunn continued, "Pecan Springs Elementary School has won first place in the elementary school division of the district-wide Science Fair for the last three years. I'm sure you've seen the trophy in the display case in the main hallway."

Cameron and Tarann exchanged smiles. She couldn't wait to get to the fifth grade so

9

she could enter a project into the Science Fair and have her name engraved on the trophy.

"Until now, the competition has been open only to our fifth- and sixth-grade students. But this year, our school district has decided that fourth-grade students can enter the Science Fair, too."

"Yeah!" Tarann shouted. She bounced up and down in her seat.

Mrs. Nunn continued, "The district has decided to accept projects from fourth-grade student teams or individual students. If you want to enter the contest with a partner, you need to fill out a special entry form. Please take a few minutes to decide if you want to work on your own or with someone else. If you choose a partner, get an entry form from me. You should fill it out and turn it in as soon as possible."

Miguel tapped Cameron on the shoulder. "Hey, Cameron, you can be my partner," he said.

Jessie, who sat in front of Cameron,

swung around. "Hey, Cameron, do you want to be my partner?"

Then Tarann leaned across the aisle and said, "Cameron, let's be partners, okay?"

"No, Cameron is going to work with me," Jessie whispered. "We've been best friends for a long time."

"But Cameron has been my best friend since I came here last year," Miguel said.

"That's nothing," Jessie said. "I've been Cameron's friend since first grade. I was his best friend first."

"No, you weren't!" Tarann said. "I've been his best friend since preschool. And I'm always his partner when we solve mysteries."

"Tarann, Jessie, and Miguel, please be quiet!" Mrs. Nunn said. "I knew I should have saved the Science Fair announcement until the end of the day. If you can't stop talking, I'm going to change your seats."

Cameron put his head in his hands. Mrs. Nunn didn't know it, but for the first time, he was happy she made everyone stop talking. Now he wouldn't have to give anyone an answer. Not now, at least. Whew.

Mrs. Nunn cleared her throat, "Okay, everyone. Please take out your English books and your homework."

Everyone took out their books. Papers rattled and pencils tapped against the desks as the class prepared their assignments for Mrs. Nunn to check.

"Where are your English book and homework, Cameron?" Mrs. Nunn asked as she walked by his desk.

"I'm sorry. I left them at home," Cameron said.

Mrs. Nunn peered at Cameron over her glasses.

"Cameron, you're in the fourth grade," she said. "You have more responsibilities now. It's important to come to class prepared."

Mrs. Nunn walked to a stack of books in the back of the class. "Come and get a book, Cameron." She wrote *Property of Mrs. Ruby Nunn's fourth-grade class* inside the cover.

Cameron hurried to get the book from

Mrs. Nunn, then sat back down at his desk. Tarann, Jessie, and Miguel all passed him notes asking him to be their Science Fair partner. Cameron put the notes inside his desk. He knew he'd have to make a choice. But who?

2
The Case of the Missing Trophy

By lunchtime, Cameron had figured out a way to choose a partner without making anyone angry. He took the notes from Miguel, Jessie, and Tarann and put them into an empty cup.

"Okay," Cameron said, "I'm going to close my eyes and pick a note out of this cup. That will be the person who will be my Science Fair partner."

"That's a good idea," Miguel said.

"I guess that's fair," Jessie said.

"Go ahead and pick a note," Tarann said.

Cameron closed his eyes and reached inside the cup. When he opened his eyes, he saw Tarann's neat handwriting.

"Hooray! We're going to be partners," Tarann said.

"Well, Miguel and I will team up, then," Jessie said. "It'll be fun."

"That sounds like a good idea," Cameron said. He was happy that he was going to do the science project with Tarann. After all, they had been partners many times before. He liked working with her.

Cameron really wanted to win the Science Fair. Everyone at school wanted to have his or her name engraved on the trophy. It was the coolest-looking trophy Cameron had ever seen. The winner of the Science Fair also got to go to Space Discovery Summer Camp and spend a month training to be a junior astronaut. Cameron had always wanted to go inside a real rocket ship.

After lunch, Cameron asked Mrs. Nunn if he could get a drink of water. He took a quick drink at the fountain and then walked to the other end of the hall near the principal's office to admire the Science Fair trophy. Two boys stopped next to him.

"Hey, kid, the trophy looks great, doesn't it?" the taller one with the wire-rimmed glasses said.

"Yes, it's huge," Cameron said.

"It's really cool, isn't it?" the other boy said, his braces glinting. "Get a good look — this trophy belongs to us."

"It belongs to the school," Cameron said.

The boy wearing braces pointed to the trophy. "If you look really close at the bottom, you'll see our names on it. Remember, sixth graders rule, right K.P.?"

"You got that right, J.W."

The boy with the braces glanced at his watch. "We'd better go. It's almost time for our meeting."

The two boys walked off laughing.

Cameron stared at the trophy. Were the two boys' names really on it? Cameron saw the names of past winners. He scanned the

list, but none of the past winners had the initials K.P. or J.W. He took his magnifying glass out of its blue plastic case to look closer at the trophy. He always had his magnifying glass with him. It came in handy.

Cameron tried to get as close as possible to the glass in order to examine it.

Suddenly, he heard a deep voice. "Hello there, little fella!"

Cameron jumped. He whirled around and saw a tall man standing behind him. Cameron had been so busy looking at the trophy, he hadn't even heard the man walk up. The man wore a huge belt buckle with a horse design on it, cowboy boots, and a brown cowboy hat.

"Didn't mean to scare you," the man said. "Take a good look at that trophy, because it's coming home with me."

The man tapped the lock on the trophy case with his finger. Then he disappeared down the hall.

Why did so many people feel that they

owned this trophy? And who was the strange man in the cowboy hat?

Cameron squeezed his face as close to the glass as he could. He could easily read the large print on the trophy. It listed the past winners, the year each winner won the Science Fair, and the school that each winner attended. But Cameron couldn't read the small print engraved on the next few lines, no matter how hard he tried. He had his face so close that he left a smudge from his forehead and nose on the glass. He tried to clean the glass with his shirtsleeve. Then he stepped back to admire the trophy again.

It had some scratches, but it looked beautiful to Cameron. No wonder everyone wanted to have their name on it. Cameron smiled. Now that he had Tarann as a partner, they very well could win. Cameron's daydream was interrupted by the janitor.

"Cameron Thompson, why on earth are you standing in front of the trophy case instead of sitting in your classroom where you belong?" Mr. Murray asked.

"I was getting some water," Cameron said.

"The water fountain isn't even on this end of the hall, son. This is the third time this month I've caught you staring at this trophy during class time. Now go back to your classroom."

Cameron hurried to class wondering about the sixth-grade boys and the strange cowboy. Who was he, anyway? There was no way he could be a part of the Science Fair. Or could he?

The next morning, Cameron was going over his Science Fair notes with Tarann. She had done some research on gravitropism and phototropism. Cameron didn't even know what the words meant until Tarann explained them to him. Gravitropism is the response of a plant to gravity, and phototropism is the response of a plant to light.

"If you grow plants and tilt them in different directions, they'll all still grow in an upward direction, opposite the force of gravity," Tarann explained. "And if you shine a light at different angles, the plants will bend toward the light."

Tarann told Cameron that every day they would record in a logbook everything they observed about the plants' reaction to gravity and light. Then they would take photos of the plants with Tarann's digital camera.

Tarann and Cameron had already finished filling out the form to enter their project in the Science Fair. Only two fourth-grade teams would be chosen to represent the school. There was a lot of competition for those two spots, but Tarann and Cameron felt confident about their project.

Suddenly, Mr. Garcia buzzed the classroom over the loudspeaker.

"Mrs. Nunn, please send Cameron Thompson to my office immediately."

"What did you do now?" Tarann whispered.

"Nothing!" Cameron said.

Mr. Garcia didn't sound too happy. That wasn't a good sign.

"Well, I hope so," Tarann said, "because we only have fifteen minutes before English to work on our project. I need you to photograph the plants at least three times a day. I've already done more than half of the work by planning and setting up the project."

"I know," Cameron said, "but that's because you picked a project that I don't know anything about."

"Cameron," Mrs. Nunn said, "you heard Mr. Garcia. Why are you talking? Go to the office now."

"I'm sorry, Mrs. Nunn," Cameron said.

Cameron headed to the office. He didn't feel good about this. What did Mr. Garcia want?

Mr. Murray was walking out of Mr. Garcia's office when Cameron arrived. He patted Cameron on the shoulder. "Sorry, son," he said.

"Sorry?" Cameron said. "What do you

mean?" But before Mr. Murray could explain, Mr. Garcia said, "Okay, Cameron. Come with me."

Cameron was puzzled. Something strange was happening.

Cameron followed Mr. Garcia into his office.

"Sit down, Cameron," Mr. Garcia said.

Cameron sat down in a wooden chair in front of Mr. Garcia's desk. His feet dangled a few inches from the floor.

"Do you have something to tell me?" Mr. Garcia asked.

"Uh, no, sir," Cameron said.

Mr. Garcia cleared his throat and sat down. "No? I don't want to call your parents, Cameron."

Cameron didn't have any idea what he was talking about.

"Are you going to tell me, Cameron, or do I have to call your parents?" Mr. Garcia asked.

"I don't know what you're talking about, Mr. Garcia."

"Really?" Mr. Garcia said. "Didn't Mr.

Murray see you in front of the trophy case yesterday?"

Cameron sighed. "Oh, so that's what you're talking about."

Mr. Murray must have told Mr. Garcia that he had seen Cameron in the hall for the third time this month without a pass again.

"Go on," Mr. Garcia said. "What do you have to say for yourself?"

"I'm sorry I was lingering in the hall," Cameron said.

"Cameron, this is no time to play games," Mr. Garcia said. "Do you know what this is?" Mr. Garcia held up a blue plastic case.

"Yes, it's a magnifying-glass case. I have one just like it."

"So, you're saying that this one isn't yours?" asked Mr. Garcia.

Cameron shook his head. "No, sir," he said. "I left mine in my pants' pocket last night. It's at my mom's house."

Cameron knew he'd left his magnifying glass at home because Tarann had asked

24

him to check the leaves on one of their plants this morning. When he couldn't find his magnifying glass, he realized that he had left it in his pocket. He was sure of that.

"This isn't like you, Cameron," Mr. Garcia said. "You see, I know this case belongs to you."

"No, sir, honest. My case and my magnifying glass are at home in the jeans I had on yesterday," Cameron said.

Cameron wondered what on earth was going on. Why would Mr. Garcia call his father about his magnifying-glass case?

Mr. Garcia stood up, clutching the case in his hand. "Do you see this scribble on the back of the case, Cameron?" He held the case so Cameron could see it.

Cameron stared at it.

"What does that say?" asked Mr. Garcia.

Cameron read the words and swallowed hard. "It says Cameron Thompson, sir."

"So it's yours, isn't it?" asked Mr. Garcia.

For a second, Cameron felt a little embarrassed. These days, it seemed like he was always leaving something behind or losing something.

"I guess you're right, Mr. Garcia," Cameron said. "It's my case. But I really did think I left it at home. I guess I was wrong."

Now Cameron wondered where his magnifying glass was. He thought it was in his pants' pocket at home, but maybe Mr. Garcia had it, too.

"Now that we have that straight, where is it, Cameron?" Mr. Garcia asked, tapping the case against the palm of his hand.

Cameron stared at Mr. Garcia. "Where is *what*?" asked Cameron. This conversation was getting weirder and weirder.

"The Science Fair trophy," said Mr. Garcia. "I don't want to play games, Cameron. I'll let you explain to your father what you've done with it."

3
The Mystery-Solving Squad

Cameron jumped up. "I didn't take the trophy, honest!" he said. "Please don't call my dad."

Mr. Garcia held the telephone receiver in his hand. "Son, if you didn't take the trophy, who did?"

"I don't know who took it, honest," Cameron said. "I was looking at the names on the trophy through my magnifying glass. I must have dropped my case."

Mr. Garcia hung up the telephone. "But Mr. Murray found the empty case in the

27

same spot where the trophy once stood. How do you explain that?" he asked.

"I don't know how to explain it," Cameron said. And he didn't know. He thought he had put the case back into his pocket. Maybe it had slipped out. But that didn't explain how it got inside the trophy case.

Mr. Garcia said, "The lock wasn't broken. Whoever took the trophy had a key."

"But I don't have a key," Cameron said.

"Yes, but I remember you telling me once that because your dad is a detective he has some kind of tool that could open most locks."

"He does," Cameron said, "but I don't have it."

"All the evidence points to you, Cameron. I need to at least discuss this with your dad. If this is some kind of prank, it could really cost the school. We've won this trophy for the past three years. And the National Science Council is coming next Monday to take pictures of our past winners and this year's participants. We have to find that trophy."

"Please, Mr. Garcia, let me work on the case for a few days," Cameron pleaded. "I'm a good detective. Remember when you thought I'd painted graffiti on the wall because you saw me with the spray-paint cans?"

Mr. Garcia nodded.

"Tarann and I solved that spray-paint mystery," said Cameron.

"Okay, Cameron," Mr. Garcia said. "But I can give you only until the end of the week. I need to know what happened to the trophy by the end of the day on Friday. If the trophy isn't back in that case by then, our school will be the laughingstock of the district."

"I'll do my very best, Mr. Garcia," Cameron said.

"Okay," Mr. Garcia said, "but remember, today is Tuesday."

Cameron nodded. "May I go now, sir?" he asked.

"Yes," said Mr. Garcia.

Cameron had no clue how he would solve this case in three days. First, he needed to examine the crime scene. If he could figure out how the thief got into the trophy case, then he'd have a clue about who took the trophy. He also needed to find the two sixth graders who told him that their names were on the trophy. And what about the man with the cowboy hat? Cameron had a lot of suspects but no clues, and only three days to solve the mystery.

Cameron walked to the trophy case and looked at it from top to bottom. A small, metal sign near the trophy read, *Donated by the Evans Family, 1965.*

He stooped down, looking for anything suspicious on the floor. He walked from one end of the case to the other, squatting and waddling like a duck. He hoped that no one saw him. He didn't have time to answer questions.

He didn't see anything but a few scuff marks in front of the case. His dad always said that sometimes the human eye can miss vital clues. That's why police take photos of crime scenes. His dad should know! He was a detective in the Austin Police Department.

Wait, that was it! Cameron needed photos of the crime scene from different angles. And he needed them before the lunch bell rang and a sea of students flowed into the hall and destroyed any evidence that might be near the trophy case.

Cameron rushed back to Mrs. Nunn's class. He needed Tarann to take photos of the crime scene with her digital camera.

"Are you in trouble, Cameron?" Mrs. Nunn asked, looking up from the papers she was checking. "Mr. Garcia sounded a little upset."

"No, I'm not in trouble, Mrs. Nunn," Cameron said.

He waited until Mrs. Nunn returned to checking her papers before whispering, "Hey, Tarann, I need you to go take a photo of the trophy case and anything near it right now. Just ask Mrs. Nunn if you can get some water. Try to take pictures from every angle."

Tarann kept reading as though she hadn't heard Cameron.

Miguel leaned forward. "What happened?" he asked.

Cameron said, "I'll tell you in a minute."

"Tarann, did you hear me?" Cameron said. "I need your help. Just tell Mrs. Nunn you want a drink. Stick the camera in your purse."

Tarann read on, dramatically wetting her finger to flip a page in her book.

Jessie said, "Tell us. What's up?"

Cameron said, "In a minute," to both Jessie and Miguel. Then he turned back to Tarann. "Tarann, I know you hear me. Please," he said.

Jessie said, "It's always all about Tarann. If you don't want to tell us what's going on, then we're no longer friends."

Miguel said, "Yeah, he's right. You always choose Tarann over us. I'm not going to be your friend anymore. And I'm not sharing my empanadas at lunch, either."

Cameron almost lost focus for a moment when Miguel said no more empanadas. Empanadas were the fried pies that Miguel's mother made. They were Cameron's favorite. But Cameron knew that Miguel and Jessie didn't mean it. They loved to tease Cameron about his friendship with Tarann.

"Tarann, I need your help. We've got another mystery to solve," Cameron pleaded. "We've got to get on the case right now."

Tarann wet her finger and flipped another page. She cleared her throat.

"Tarann, please," Miguel said, mocking Cameron.

Jessie said, "Why do you keep begging her when you see she's not listening?"

Cameron felt desperate. Cameron whispered as loud as he dared, "Tarann!"

"Cameron, why are you talking?" Mrs. Nunn asked. "Do you want to go to the principal's office again?"

"No, Mrs. Nunn," Cameron said. "I just need to tell Tarann something important."

"Okay, you have two minutes. I hope it's about your science project."

Cameron sighed with relief. He leaned over to Tarann and spoke to her as fast as he could. "I'm in trouble. The Science Fair trophy is missing, and Mr. Garcia thinks I took it, but I didn't. So now I have to figure out who did. I only have three days."

"That's too bad," Tarann said, talking even faster. "Because I've decided that you don't care whether we win the Science Fair or not. And you know exactly how much I'd like to win. As soon as we started working this morning, Mr. Garcia called you to his office. I already feel like I'm doing most of the work."

Cameron looked at the clock. His two minutes were almost up. "Please, I'm sorry. I'll pull my weight from now on," Cameron said.

"Promise?" Tarann asked.

"I promise," Cameron said.

"Quick," Tarann said, "what do you want me to take a picture of?"

"All angles of the trophy case," said Cameron.

"Okay. I'll do it. But you have to tell me the whole story at lunch," said Tarann.

"Sure, and I'll tell Miguel and Jessie, too," Cameron said, loud enough for his friends to hear him.

Tarann raised her hand, "Mrs. Nunn, may I have a pass, please? I need to take care of something really important."

"Of course," Mrs. Nunn said.

That's what Cameron admired most about Tarann. She believed in always telling the truth, no matter what happened.

Mrs. Nunn said, "It's time for math, everyone. Take out your math books, please."

Cameron watched Tarann leave the room with her camera. Then he pulled out his math book and started working on the problems.

At lunch, Cameron told Tarann, Miguel, and Jessie everything that had happened.

"Three days isn't a very long time to solve a mystery," Miguel said.

"I think I might need more help," Cameron said. "This might be a job for the Mystery-Solving Squad."

"Who are they?" Jessie asked.

Cameron smiled, "Tarann, Miguel, you, and me, that's who. Do you want to be on the team?"

"We're in," Miguel said quickly.

"All for one, and one for all," Jessie said, swishing his arm through the air like a swordsman.

"Except we solve mysteries," Cameron said, "so we're the Mystery-Solving Squad."

"I like that," Tarann said.

"So do I," Miguel said.

"Then it's settled," Cameron said. "Now let's get to work. Tarann, let's see the photos you took."

Tarann opened her purse and handed Cameron her digital camera.

Cameron looked at the photos on the small screen on the back of the digital camera. He didn't see anything out of place except the open trophy case and the empty space where the trophy had once been.

"Take a look, Miguel and Jessie," Cameron said. Cameron's dad had always told him that it was important to have a fresh pair of eyes on a case. Someone else might spot something you've missed.

"I don't see anything," Miguel said. "What about you, Jessie? Do you see anything?"

Jessie stared at the photos.

"Nope. Not a thing," he said.

"I'll print the pictures when I get home," Tarann said. "Maybe you'll be able to find some clues when you look at the larger photos."

"Thanks," Cameron said. "I'll find my magnifying glass when I get home and examine them a little closer tomorrow."

4
Two Suspects

By the last lesson of the day, Cameron was exhausted. He needed a nap, and he hadn't wanted one since he was about four years old!

"Cameron, we have a problem," Tarann said.

"What?" Cameron asked.

"Someone knocked over one of our science project plants. We need to set it up again."

"You have to be kidding," Cameron said. This was turning out to be a terrible day.

Cameron and Tarann worked together to place the plant back into the pot and get it back into position under the light. Then they took pictures of the plants, recorded their observations in their logbook, and measured the angle of each stem, using a protractor.

Cameron realized that it was difficult to keep up with everything. They were supposed to take turns photographing and measuring the plants three times a day, but Cameron hadn't managed to do his part.

He really wanted to pull his weight. But since his mother moved back to Austin, it hadn't been easy keeping everything straight. No one seemed to realize how much stuff Cameron had to carry from one house to the other.

When the bell rang, Cameron and the Mystery-Solving Squad filed out of Mrs. Nunn's class and gathered around Cameron's locker.

"We've got to find out who the two boys are who stopped to talk to me when I was

looking at the trophy," Cameron said. "I know they're in the sixth grade. Here are their descriptions," Cameron said, handing a sheet of paper to each of his friends.

Jessie read the description. "*A boy with braces.* This could be anybody."

"He's right," Miguel said. "And what about this one: *A tall boy with glasses.* Do you have any idea how many tall boys in this school wear glasses?"

"Come on, Cameron," Tarann said. "Your dad taught you how to be a good witness. You told me so."

Tarann was right. Cameron closed his eyes.

"Write this down. Okay, they told me their initials. Let me think. I remember looking for the initials carved on the trophy. My dad says you should make associations in your mind when you want to remember something. I remember thinking that one boy's initials reminded me of something in the army."

"Camouflage?" Miguel asked.

"No, something that actually sounded like his initials. Wait, wait, I know! K.P. My dad talks about when he had to do K.P. in the army. I think it means cooking or something. The initials of the boy with glasses are . . . K.P. And he wore a button-down dress shirt. I remember wondering if he had on a tie for something special at school."

"Okay," Tarann said. "Can you think of anything else about his face, his hair, or something like that?"

"Hmmm. I don't know. I was paying more attention to the guy with the braces."

"What do you remember about the guy with the braces?" Jessie asked.

"I remember that he was wearing brown suede lace-ups with a gold design on them," said Cameron.

"That's good. If he had on those shoes, he probably always wears them. Now that's a good description," Tarann said, excitedly.

"Now we're beginning to sound like real

detectives," Cameron said. "Oh, wait. I do remember one more thing." Cameron remembered the boy with the braces pointing at the trophy. "He was wearing a Space Invaders watch," he said.

"Well, that should narrow down our search," Jessie said. "Not that many people wear that kind of watch."

"We only have three days, guys. We've got to get cracking on this case," Tarann said.

"Well, I've got to go home now," Jessie said.

"Me, too," said Miguel. "But can we meet later to talk about the case?"

"I can't," Cameron said. "My mom wants to spend some time with me. I was at my dad's last week and she wants to cook a special dinner and play games and stuff tonight."

"Okay, maybe we can all talk on the phone then," Tarann said.

"Good idea! I can use my mom's phone to make a conference call to everyone. That way, we can all talk about the case at the same time," said Cameron.

"Great!" Jessie said.

"Oops, it's getting late," Cameron said. "I've got to get going. My mom's picking me up in front of school. See you later."

"'Bye," Tarann said. "Don't forget to call us."

Cameron spotted his mom's car directly in front of the school's walkway. There was a crowd of people still in the schoolyard. Cameron hoped his mom remembered the new "no kissing and hugging in public" rule. If she forgot, he'd just have to gently push her away if she tried to kiss his "pudgy-wudgy little cheeks."

Cameron hopped into the car and put on his seat belt.

"Hey, Mom," Cameron said.

"Hello, son," his mother said.

She didn't lean over to kiss and hug him like she usually did. Cameron held out his hand. His mother smiled and shook it as if she were closing a business deal.

"I hope you had a good day at school. What did you do today?" his mom asked.

For a second, Cameron felt nervous. Had Mr. Garcia called to tell her what happened? He hoped not.

"Cameron," his mom said, starting the engine of the car. "Did you hear me? What did you do today, baby? I mean, son?"

Cameron decided that if his mother didn't know about the missing trophy, it would be better if she heard everything from him. He took a deep breath.

"I have a problem, Mom," said Cameron.

"I hope you're not having trouble with your grades," she said. "You've done so well lately."

"No, it's not exactly about my schoolwork. Well, it is, sort of. See, Tarann and I want to win the Science Fair."

"That's wonderful!" his mother said. "I'm glad to see you're taking an interest in science. That was my favorite subject in high school."

"Well, we think we have a great project,"

Cameron said. "But the trophy is missing. Monday night, someone unlocked the case and took it. Mr. Murray saw me in front of the trophy case that day and told Mr. Garcia. At first he thought I took the trophy because they found my magnifying-glass case in the display case. But I explained that I didn't have anything to do with it. So I asked Mr. Garcia if I could try to solve the mystery of the missing trophy. He gave me until Friday."

"Well, I know you had nothing to do with it. And if anyone can figure it out, you can," his mother said. "I was so proud of the way you solved that spray-paint mystery last year."

"Thanks, Mom," Cameron said.

"Come on," his mom said as they pulled into the driveway. "I've fixed a big pot of stew and a pan of corn bread for dinner. You can make the salad."

Cameron explained all the details of the missing trophy that night at dinner.

"You know your dad is the best detective

in Austin," his mom said. "I'm sure you've inherited his skills. I have a hunch you'll figure out a way to identify those sixth graders before you fall asleep tonight. Now wash the dishes, young man. Then we'll play a game."

"Mom, can I make a conference call to the Mystery-Solving Squad after I wash the dishes? I need to talk to them before it gets too late."

"That's fine," his mom said. "Just let me know when you're finished and I'll set up the game board."

Cameron quickly washed the dishes so he could make the phone call. Then he went into his mother's office and dialed Tarann, Miguel, and Jessie. When everyone was on the line, he started to talk.

"I think we need to find out who those sixth graders are first," Cameron said. "Then we'll need to find out everything we can about them. We also need to find out who that man in the cowboy hat is."

"We can use the descriptions you gave us," Jessie said, "but those two guys are going to be hard to find if that's all we've got to go on."

"We'll do the best we can," Miguel said.

"Thanks, guys," Cameron said. "Tarann, I need you to bring the photos to school tomorrow so I can look at them again."

"I've already printed them out and put them in my backpack," Tarann said.

"Great," Cameron said.

"Listen, I have a way to ID those sixth graders really fast," Jessie said.

"How?" Miguel asked.

"Our school yearbook from last year. They would've been in fifth grade. All you have to do is check out the fifth-grade classes and find their photos. I bet they were even in the Science Club."

"That's a super idea," Tarann said. "I should've thought of that."

"That's why it's good to have a team working on this case," Cameron said. "Four heads are better than one."

"Look through your yearbook tonight and see if you can find them," Jessie said.

"Okay," Cameron said. "Let's get to school early tomorrow and meet at our lockers."

"Great plan," Tarann said. "See you all tomorrow!"

After everyone said good-bye and hung up, Cameron went into the living room to find his mother. She had a checkerboard set up on the coffee table.

After three quick games, it was time for Cameron to get ready for bed.

"Okay, son," his mom said. "Hit the shower and get everything ready for school in the morning."

"Okay, Mom," Cameron said. He went upstairs to his room, took a quick shower, and put on his pajamas. Then Cameron lay in bed, thinking about the case. He got out of bed and walked over to his bookshelf. Luckily, most of his schoolwork, photos, and books from last year were at his mother's house. She had been saving everything of Cameron's since he was a baby. For once, Cameron was glad his mother didn't throw anything away.

He hurried to find his school yearbook before his mother came in to kiss him good night. He thumbed through the pages, carefully examining each photo.

Cameron knew that to solve a crime, it's important to work slowly. His dad always told him that you can miss valuable information if you're not patient enough. Cameron looked through the entire yearbook, but he didn't find a fifth-grade boy who wore braces or one wearing glasses who looked familiar.

Cameron put the yearbook down and searched through a pile of his dirty clothes for the pants he wore yesterday. He needed his magnifying glass. He pulled it out of the front pocket and put the dirty clothes back into the hamper.

He used his magnifying glass to reexamine the pictures. Cameron thought that maybe the boy who wore glasses didn't have them the year before. Or maybe he took them off before the class picture was taken.

Maybe the boy who wore braces didn't smile in the picture so the braces wouldn't show. Cameron knew a lot of kids who didn't smile for pictures after they got their braces.

As he flipped the pages, he found two boys who looked similar to his suspects. Cameron took a pencil out of his desk drawer. He lightly drew a pair of glasses on a boy who looked like one of his suspects. He recognized him immediately.

"Gotcha!" Cameron said.

The boy was in a group photo. His name was Kenneth Parker. Cameron looked carefully at the boy standing next to Kenneth Parker. It was the boy who had the braces. He wasn't smiling in any of the pictures.

Cameron moved the magnifying glass closer to the second boy's wrist. He was wearing a Space Invaders watch.

Cameron looked at the names under the photo for the name of the second boy. It was Jeff Watson, and he was president of the Science Club.

"K.P. and J.W.," Cameron whispered, "I gotcha!"

Cameron's mom tapped on his door. "It's time for bed, son. But make sure you straighten up that messy desk first."

"I will, Mom," Cameron said as he closed the yearbook and put it inside his backpack. He couldn't wait to show the rest of the team what he'd discovered.

Cameron stacked the papers on his desk and put his books back on the bookshelf. Then he got into bed. He couldn't stop thinking about the missing trophy or all the clues he had uncovered. He had to find out who took that trophy.

Cameron's mom walked back into the room. She smiled when she saw the neatly stacked papers on his desk. When it came to neatness, Cameron's mom and dad were alike.

"That's better, son," his mom said. "And you even picked up your clothes without being asked. Good job!"

"Thanks, Mom," Cameron said. "Oh,

yeah, you were right about figuring things out before bedtime. I found the boys I saw by the trophy case in my yearbook."

"Good detective work, Cameron," his mother said as she gave him a peck on the forehead.

Cameron gave her a hug. He didn't mind being hugged and kissed as long as no one was around to see it. His mom switched off the light and went into her room.

Cameron snuggled under the covers. He felt proud of the fact that he had figured out the identities of two of his suspects. But how was he going to find a way to question Jeff Watson and Kenneth Parker about the missing trophy without making them suspicious?

5
Cameron Thompson, Super Detective

As planned, Cameron and his friends met before school in front of their lockers. Cameron showed everyone the pictures he had found in the yearbook, and Tarann gave him the copies of the digital photos she had taken of the empty trophy case.

"These are great, Tarann," Cameron said. "Thanks."

"You're welcome," Tarann said. "Hopefully you'll discover a clue that will help us find the trophy."

"Jessie," Cameron said, "I want you to

ask around and get the scoop on Jeff Watson, alias J.W. And, Miguel, I want you to find out about Kenneth Parker. He's K.P."

"Well," Tarann said, "they're both in the Science Club. Maybe we should go to a meeting and talk to them afterward. That would be one way to find out about them."

"That's a great idea!" Cameron said with a smile. "And being Science Club members will help us with our Science Fair projects. They're having a meeting today after school. We should stay and check it out."

"That's a good idea, but Jessie and I have something to tell you about the Science Fair," Miguel said.

"What?" Cameron asked.

"We've decided to try out for the math team instead," Jessie said. "So we're dropping out of the Science Fair."

"That's fine," Cameron said. "Now I won't have to compete against two of my best friends."

"So, what else do we need to investigate?" Miguel asked.

"I'm going to go back to the trophy case and look it over really carefully at lunchtime," Cameron said. "There has to be a clue I haven't found yet."

"Maybe if you compare the photos from yesterday with the way the trophy case looks now, something will stand out," Jessie said.

"Good idea," Cameron said. "Tarann, you and I will do that at lunchtime. Now we all have our assignments."

"All for one," Jessie said.

"And one for all," the others said.

Everyone laughed. The bell rang, and they went into class.

The morning flew by. When the lunch bell rang, Cameron and his friends set off to investigate.

"Okay, the sixth graders eat lunch at the same time we do," Miguel said. "That'll give Jessie and me a chance to ask around about Jeff and Ken."

"Tarann and I will check out the trophy case," Cameron said. "We'll meet you in the lunchroom and compare notes."

"See you later," Jessie said, and he and Miguel headed off.

Cameron and Tarann went to the trophy case. Cameron took out the photos that Tarann had taken the morning after the trophy was stolen. They carefully compared the photos to the way the case looked now.

"It looks the same to me. Now what?" Tarann asked.

"We've got to find a clue," Cameron said. "We're missing something. Something that's in the pictures, but we just haven't seen it yet," Cameron said.

"The lock isn't broken. Whoever took the trophy definitely had a key," Tarann said as she looked closely at the keyhole.

"That's true," Cameron said. "Maybe they took the key out of the office when no one was looking. Let me look at the photos again with my magnifying glass," Cameron said.

Tarann looked over his shoulder. "What are you looking for? We've looked at these pictures about a million times."

"Just give me a minute," Cameron said as he carefully examined the photos.

Something had been nagging at Cameron since the first day he saw the photos. In them, there was a short line of faint black marks on the floor in front of the case. That was it!

"There it is!" Cameron said, pointing at the bottom of the photograph.

"What?" Tarann asked.

"Tread marks. They're hard to see without the magnifying glass, but they're there. What makes tread marks like that?" asked Cameron.

"I don't know," Tarann said. "Maybe they're from a shoe or something."

"No," Cameron said. "They're not from a shoe. This photo shows a long row of black marks, side by side. Shoes would leave uneven marks."

"Maybe they were made by one of the book carts like the ones they use in the library," Tarann said.

"No, those have four wheels that are spaced apart. It would leave marks that are wider apart. These marks are pretty close together." Cameron thought for a minute. "I know what made these marks!" he said. "A dolly. You know, like the one Mr. Murray uses to move furniture. It has two rubber wheels and a little piece of metal that you can carry things on. You put something heavy on it, then tip it back so you can move it."

"So that's what made the black marks in front of the trophy case?" Tarann asked.

"I think so," Cameron said.

"And the marks were made because the weight of the trophy made the black rubber wheels rub against the floor," said Tarann. "This is one of the best clues we've had in a long time."

"And the front hall goes directly to the back door of the school where the loading dock is!" said Cameron.

"Do you think the thief got the dolly from the loading dock?" Tarann asked.

"I don't know," Cameron said, "but I'm going to find out. Mr. Murray will know if they keep a dolly there."

"Let's find him," Tarann said. "I'll bet he's in the lunchroom."

"Let's go," Cameron said. "Because I'm hungry, too."

When they walked in, Mr. Murray was wiping off one of the empty tables.

"Excuse me, Mr. Murray. We have some questions we need to ask you," Cameron said.

"What can I help you with?" Mr. Murray said.

"Are you missing a dolly from the loading dock?" Tarann asked.

"Yes!" Mr. Murray said. "How did you know that? I was looking for it earlier today. I thought maybe I might have left it in one of the classrooms. Did you find it?"

"No, sir," Cameron said. "We think someone took it to move the trophy."

"Come to think of it," Mr. Murray said, "I

haven't used that dolly since last Friday. I usually leave it on the dock until I need it."

"Someone took the trophy between Monday afternoon and Tuesday morning," Tarann said. "So this may explain how it was moved. But we still don't know how they got a key to the case."

"Well, that trophy case is as old as the school," Mr. Murray said. "That lock wouldn't be hard to open with a nail file or some other sharp instrument."

"Thanks, Mr. Murray," Cameron said. "That information helps us a lot."

"You're welcome," Mr. Murray said. "Good luck with the case. I know you'll solve the mystery. You're great detectives."

"Thanks, Mr. Murray," Cameron said with a smile.

Tarann and Cameron got their lunch and sat down with Jessie and Miguel to discuss the case.

"What did you find out?" Cameron asked between bites of his lunch.

"Well, it turns out that my brother, Duran, is in the same class as Jeff Watson," Jessie said. "Duran says that he's one of the smartest boys in sixth grade. He lives a few blocks from school in that big blue house on the corner."

"Jeff's brother is in high school now. He won the trophy when he was in sixth grade," Miguel said. "And Jeff's father won it when he went to this school, too. It's like Jeff has to keep up the family tradition and win the Science Fair trophy this year."

"What about Ken Parker?" Cameron asked. "Did you find out anything about him?"

"Yes," Miguel said. "Duran said that Ken lives just a few blocks from you. And he's always hanging out with Jeff Watson."

"Maybe they took the trophy together," Cameron said. "What we need to know is why."

"One thing's for sure," Jessie said. "I think that it would take more than one kid to move the trophy out of the case. That thing is huge."

"Well, we found out that the school's dolly is missing," Tarann said. "They could move it pretty easily with the dolly."

"But why would someone want to take the trophy?" Cameron asked. "And why did the man in the cowboy hat say the trophy was going home with him?"

"I don't know. It doesn't make sense," Jessie said. "The sixth graders I talked to all say that Jeff's been bragging that he's going to win the Science Fair this year. So why would he want to take the trophy?"

"The Science Club meets this afternoon. Maybe we can talk to Jeff and Ken and get some clues," Cameron said.

The bell rang. "Tarann, let's meet after school," Cameron said. "We can call our parents and tell them we're going to walk home together after the Science Club meeting. Then we can walk past Ken's house and see if we notice anything suspicious."

"Good idea," Tarann said.

"Sounds like a plan to me," Miguel said.

"Okay," Cameron said. "Let's meet in front of the lockers again in the morning to report what we find out."

"Will do," Jessie said. "All for one!"

"And one for all," everyone said.

As soon as school was over for the day, Cameron called his mother.

"Mom, do you think I could walk home with Tarann today?" Cameron asked. "We're going to a Science Club meeting after school."

"Okay," Cameron's mom said. "But make sure you get home before four-thirty. Remember, it's your turn to start dinner. And don't get into any trouble."

"I won't, Mom. I'm not a baby anymore."

"I know that," his mom said. "I was the one changing all those diapers, remember?"

"Funny, Mom," Cameron said. "I'll see you later."

Tarann was waiting for Cameron in the hallway. The Science Club was meeting in Mr. Robinson's sixth-grade classroom.

"Hello, there," Mr. Robinson said. "You're new to the club, aren't you?"

"Yes, sir," Cameron said.

"We'd like to sign up," Tarann said.

"Very good," Mr. Robinson said. "Just take these forms home for your parents to sign."

Tarann and Cameron took seats at the back of the classroom. Jeff Watson, the Science Club president, stood in the front of the room. Twelve other kids, mostly sixth graders, sat close to the front.

"I have an announcement to make before I begin the meeting," Jeff said. "As you all know, last year Ken and I worked as partners on an astronomy project and we won Honorable Mention at the Science Fair."

Everyone applauded. Ken Parker stared angrily at the floor.

"Ken looks like he's upset about something," Tarann whispered to Cameron.

"Maybe they had an argument," Cameron said.

Jeff held up his hands for everyone to be quiet.

"This year, I've decided to work alone," Jeff said. "I made my decision on Monday. I want to try for first place on my own. I know this is a surprise to most of you, but I wish everyone good luck."

Ken quickly left the room. Tarann and Cameron exchanged a look. They followed Ken outside.

"Ken, wait a minute," Cameron said. "We want to talk to you."

"What do you want?" Ken asked.

"I saw you and Jeff on Monday when I was looking at the Science Fair trophy," Cameron said.

"Yeah, I remember you," Ken said. "Right after that, Jeff told me that we wouldn't be partners."

"Did you know that the Science Fair trophy is missing?" asked Tarann.

"Yes," Ken said, smiling slightly. "I guess Jeff won't get his name on that trophy after all, will he?" Ken looked toward the door. "I've got to go home now."

Cameron and Tarann watched Ken walk down the hall. He got his books out of his locker and slammed the door shut. Then he pushed his way through the double doors that led outside.

"Do you think he took the trophy and hid it at his house?" Tarann asked.

"I don't know," Cameron said, "but let's follow him. I want to watch his house for a while and see if we see anything suspicious. I don't have too much time. My mom wants me to start dinner tonight."

"Let me guess," Tarann said. "I'll bet you're cooking spaghetti."

"Of course," Cameron said. "My mom loves my spaghetti."

"That's a good thing," Tarann said with a smile, "since it's the only thing you can cook."

"That's true," Cameron said.

He stopped Tarann when they reached the house where Kenneth Parker lived.

"Look!" Cameron said suddenly.

Kenneth came out of the front door and walked around to the garage.

"Hide!" Cameron said. "We need to stay out of sight."

He quickly pulled Tarann behind a row of shrubs. They crouched down. The ground was muddy and covered with twigs and gravel. It wasn't a great place to sit, but it was the only way to watch Kenneth without being seen.

"What's he doing?" Tarann whispered.

"Shhh," Cameron said. "He might hear you. Take a look yourself, but don't let him see you."

Tarann peered over the top of the shrubs. She and Cameron watched Kenneth as he pulled a red wagon out of the garage. He dropped some rope into the wagon's bed. Cameron carefully pushed the shrubs apart so he could see better.

"What do you think he's doing?" Tarann asked.

"I don't know," Cameron replied, "but it

looks like he's going to move something. It must be something heavy if he needs a wagon and rope."

They looked at each other. The *trophy* was big and heavy!

Kenneth pulled the red wagon up two steps and onto the front porch. Then he looked around, as if to make sure no one was watching. Cameron and Tarann ducked behind the bushes again. They could hear Kenneth pulling the wagon into the house.

"Do you think he'll come back out?" Cameron said.

"I hope so," Tarann said. "Otherwise, we're covered in mud for nothing."

"Mud?" Cameron said. Then he looked down at his feet. His sneakers were caked with mud. The sprinkler must have been on just before they ran over behind the shrubs. Cameron lifted up his foot, but his shoe stayed put.

"Oops," he said, holding onto the bush to keep from toppling over. His shoeless foot squished into the mud.

"Shhhh. Duck! He's coming back," Tarann said.

They watched Kenneth pulling the red wagon back down the steps to the garage. Something tall and covered with a blanket was in the center of the wagon. Kenneth held on to the object with one hand and pulled the wagon down the steps with the other.

"It has to be the trophy," Tarann said. "It's about the same size and shape. What should we do?"

"Watch and wait," Cameron said, glancing down at the muddy mess that covered his shoes and sock. His mom was *not* going to be happy.

They watched Kenneth struggle to pull the wagon around to the garage. He pushed the button on the remote, and the garage door squeaked as it slowly opened. Kenneth pulled the wagon inside. He placed his hand on top of the mysterious item to hold it steady as he wheeled it into the garage.

Cameron and Tarann anxiously waited

for Kenneth to reappear. After a few minutes, he came out. He didn't have the wagon with him. He pressed a button on the remote, and the garage door creaked shut. Kenneth looked around once more and then went inside the house.

"That could be the trophy in the wagon," Tarann said as she brushed some twigs from her pants. "It's the same height for sure."

"If that's the trophy, what do you think he's going to do with it?" asked Cameron.

"I don't know," Tarann said. "We only have two more days to solve the crime. I say we turn Ken in. That way Mr. Garcia can talk to him and ask him about whatever that is in his garage. Maybe he took the trophy as a prank or to get even with Jeff or something."

"Okay, tomorrow we'll talk to Mr. Garcia," Cameron said. "I just wish we had more proof that what he put in the garage really is the trophy. I don't want to get him into trouble over nothing."

"Well, all the information we have so far points to him," Tarann said. "He's upset with Jeff because they're not going to be Science Fair partners. And he's hiding something in his garage that looks like the trophy."

"I guess you're right," Cameron said. "Except we haven't really investigated our other suspect, the man in the cowboy hat. But all the evidence so far does point to Ken."

"Well, it looks like we're on our way to solving another mystery," Tarann said. "One day they'll write a book about our adventures, I bet."

"Maybe so," Cameron said. "The title can be *Cameron Thompson, Super Detective, and His Sidekick, Tarann Johnson.*"

"What? I'm no sidekick!" Tarann said.

"Okay," Cameron said, laughing, "*Cameron Thompson, Super Detective.* Period."

"Very funny," Tarann said.

"Okay, I have to go home now," Cameron said. "I'll see you tomorrow."

"See you later, Mr. Super Detective," Tarann said.

As soon as he got to his mom's house, Cameron washed the mud off his shoes and scrubbed it off his sock with some laundry detergent. When he finished, they looked almost as good as new. Then he started making dinner. His mom would be home in an hour.

Cameron chopped up some celery and red peppers. He poured a jar of spaghetti sauce into a bowl. Then he mixed the vegetables into the sauce with a few tablespoons of salsa. Cameron stirred the sauce and put it into the microwave to cook. This was his own recipe and he was proud of it.

As soon as the water began to boil, he added the spaghetti noodles. He stirred them so the noodles wouldn't stick together. Once, when Cameron first started cooking spaghetti, he forgot to stir the noodles and they all stuck together in a huge ball. His mom poured the sauce over it and cut it into pieces with a knife. It still tasted good, but you couldn't twirl the spaghetti.

Cameron now added his famous, secret recipe spaghetti. Once the spaghetti and sauce were ready, he crumbled two pieces of toasted bread into crumbs in a bowl. He grated some cheese and mixed it in with the bread crumbs. His topping for the spaghetti was ready!

Cameron sprinkled the topping over the spaghetti and sauce. He made a salad and put everything into the refrigerator. When he was finished, Cameron went into his room to do his homework.

Cameron had several chapters to read and questions to answer in his Social Studies book. When he was done with the last question, he fell fast asleep, his face lying flat on a map of Africa. His mother gently shook him awake.

"Hey, there," his mom said. "I guess you must have had a busy day. You can tell me about your adventures during dinner. Then I think you need to go to bed early tonight, okay?"

"Okay," Cameron agreed. He was tired and tomorrow would be another busy day.

Cameron and his mom ate dinner, then they cleaned up. When Cameron finally got into bed, his mind raced. He couldn't wait to tell Jessie and Miguel about his adventure with Tarann. But he was worried about turning in Ken to Mr. Garcia. What if they were wrong? Cameron had been suspected of doing things when he had been innocent. He knew it was a terrible feeling. Cameron had a hard time falling asleep.

6
The Man with the Cowboy Hat

When Cameron got to school on Thursday morning, he spotted Tarann, Miguel, and Jessie the minute he hopped out of his mother's car. He could tell from their faces that something was wrong.

"What's the matter?" Cameron asked. "Tarann, didn't you tell them we've solved the crime?"

"Yes and no," Miguel said.

"What does that mean?" Cameron asked.

"Well, she told us you saw Kenneth Parker

smuggling the trophy out of his house into his garage, right?" Jessie said.

"Right," Cameron said. "I mean, we didn't exactly see the trophy, but whatever it was, was the same height and the right size."

"How can you accuse Ken of taking the trophy unless you know he really has it?" Miguel asked. "I think we need to do some more investigating."

"Good thinking," Cameron said. "My dad says sometimes the obvious answer is right under your nose. Maybe we're missing something, but what?"

"I think we should tell Mr. Garcia and let him figure things out," Tarann said.

"But if Ken doesn't have the trophy, we'll be reporting him for nothing," Jessie said.

"We have to tell Mr. Garcia what we saw," Tarann said. "Cameron promised that he'd find the trophy, and there's a chance that Ken might have it. Ken won't know who told Mr. Garcia."

"Let's vote on it," Cameron said. "All in

favor of telling Mr. Garcia, raise your hands."

Tarann was the only one who raised her hand.

"Why don't you want to turn him in?" Tarann asked.

"We don't really have any proof," Cameron said. "I think we should keep looking, like Miguel said. We still haven't found out about that man in the cowboy hat who I saw in the hallway. And he said he was taking the trophy home with him."

"But the only information we have is that he wears a cowboy hat," Tarann said.

"You're right," Cameron said. "How about we give it one more day before we tell Mr. Garcia? That way, we can check out the man in the cowboy hat. Then we can tell Mr. Garcia everything we did to solve the mystery."

"That's a good idea," Jessie said.

"Okay," Cameron said. "So we'll wait until tomorrow to talk to Mr. Garcia. All in favor?"

"All right," Miguel said, raising his hand.

"I agree," Jessie said, raising his hand, too.

"Okay. I'll go along with waiting," Tarann said. "Besides, we need to concentrate on our Science Fair project today. It has to be ready by tomorrow afternoon to show to the Science Fair panel. They'll be picking which fourth-grade projects are good enough to be in the district-wide Science Fair."

"We don't have much time," Cameron said. "Maybe we can work on the case at lunch. We can ask around about the man in the cowboy hat. Someone had to see him that day."

"Okay, that's the plan," Tarann said. "Now, let's go measure our plants. We'll work on our project before the morning bell rings."

"Let's go," Cameron said.

As he and Tarann measured their plants, Cameron was surprised to discover one plant growing in the weirdest direction. It was pointing like a crooked finger toward the light. It almost looked like the finger of the man in the cowboy hat when he'd pointed to the trophy. Suddenly, Cameron remembered an important clue!

"Hey, Tarann," Cameron said, "I just remembered something. The man in the cowboy hat had on a funny-looking ring."

"What do you mean by funny-looking?" asked Tarann.

"It was a big, gold square with an N in the center of it."

"The letter N?" Tarann asked.

Cameron shrugged. "That's what it looked like to me," he said.

"Maybe N is the first letter of his name," Tarann said. "How can we find out who he was?"

Cameron thought about it for a moment. "I know. We could check the visitor's sign-in book in the main office. Every visitor at the school has to sign it."

"You're right," Tarann said. "Come on, the bell's going to ring in a few minutes."

They rushed to the office. Ms. Fergins, the secretary, was talking on the telephone.

Cameron whispered to Tarann, "What if she won't let us look at it?"

Tarann said, "Why wouldn't she? It's not like it's a big secret who comes to visit our school."

Ms. Fergins hung up the phone. "How can I help you two today?"

"We'd like to take a look at the visitors' sign-in book."

"It's on the counter," Ms. Fergins said. "Help yourselves."

Cameron read the list of names of the people who visited the school on Monday. He didn't see anyone who had a first or last namc that began with N.

"Excuse me, Ms. Fergins, but do you remember seeing a man wearing a cowboy hat on Monday?"

"No, I don't believe I do," said Ms. Fergins.

"He was an older man," Cameron said, "wearing a big brown cowboy hat, a belt buckle with a horse on it, and cowboy boots."

Ms. Fergins said, "I think I would have remembered someone like that. Did you ask Mr. Murray or Mr. Garcia?"

"Not yet," Tarann said. "Is Mr. Garcia in his office?"

"No, he's out of the building at a meeting. But I think Mr. Murray is down the hall. Go talk to him, then go straight to class. I'll write a pass for you."

"Thanks, Ms. Fergins," Tarann said. "You're the best."

Cameron smiled. Tarann really knew what to say to grown-ups.

"Come on," Cameron said. "Let's find Mr. Murray."

Mr. Murray was emptying the trash at the end of the hall.

"Hi, Mr. Murray," Cameron said. "How are you today?"

"Fine, thank you," Mr. Murray said. "What can I do for you two?"

"When I was looking at the trophy on Monday, there was a man who stopped by dressed like a cowboy. Did you see him?"

"A cowboy," Mr. Murray said. "No. But you know, here in Texas, that description could fit a lot of men."

"That's true," Tarann said, "but this man was also wearing a big belt buckle with a horse on it."

"Did you check with Mr. Phillips?" Mr. Murray asked. "His fifth-grade class is studying cowboys this year. Maybe he invited a guest."

"We can check with him at lunchtime," Cameron said. "His class is in the lunchroom at the same time as ours. Thanks for the tip."

"You're welcome," Mr. Murray said. "Good luck with the case."

It was moments like these that Cameron felt like a real detective.

When he and Tarann raced into Mrs. Nunn's room, they could see she was not happy.

"Where have you two been?" Mrs. Nunn asked.

"We're very sorry we're late," Cameron

said. "But Ms. Fergins told us to talk to Mr. Murray."

"Really?" Mrs. Nunn asked, "Then where is your pass?"

"Here it is, Mrs. Nunn," Cameron said, handing her the pass.

"Okay, you're excused," Mrs. Nunn said. "Now hurry and get busy on your science project."

Tarann and Cameron went to their desks and pulled out their notebooks. They went over the information that they had collected about their plants.

"We need to make sure our data is complete," Tarann said. "We also need to make a graph."

"I'll make the graph while you work on the data. And I'll put the photos in order," Cameron said.

"Good," Tarann said. "I don't like to draw graphs."

"You don't like to draw, period," Cameron said. "I love to draw. That's why we make a good team."

Cameron neatly graphed all the information about the plants. Suddenly, he thought of a way to find the man in the cowboy hat.

"Tarann," Cameron whispered. "You just gave me an idea."

"I did? What?" Tarann asked. "I hope it has something to do with our science project. We still need to make sure the photos tell a complete story."

"Actually, no," Cameron said, feeling a little guilty. "It's about the man in the cowboy hat. Maybe I could sketch a picture of him, like a police artist does."

"That's a super idea," Tarann said. "We can make flyers and pass them out at lunch. They could say *Has anyone seen this man?* like they do in the movies."

"Yeah," Cameron said. "And we can ask people to contact the office. Then Ms. Fergins can let us know who called and we can talk to them."

"What if it doesn't work?" Tarann asked.

"It will. It has to," Cameron said. "We only have one more day."

"But how are we going to get copies of the flyers to pass out by lunchtime?" Tarann asked.

"Good question," Cameron said. "I know! Maybe my mom can do it. She's off from work today."

"That's a good idea," Tarann said. "You'd better get busy and draw that picture. I'll put the photos in order."

"Thanks, Tarann," Cameron said. He took out a clean sheet of paper and began to draw. There was only one thing in school that Cameron loved more than reading, and that was art. The school's art teacher, Miss Carter, said that he was one of the best artists in the school.

Cameron worked on his picture. He drew the man's face, the cowboy hat, and the belt buckle with the horse on it. His final touch was the gold ring with the big N on it that the mystery man had on his finger.

When Cameron finished the picture, he showed it to Tarann.

"That's great!" she said.

"Let me see what you drew," Miguel said.

Cameron passed it to Miguel.

"You're such a good artist!" said Miguel.

"I want to see it," Jessie said.

Miguel passed it to Jessie.

"Yeah, this is cool," Jessie said.

Jessie handed the picture back to Cameron. Then Cameron wrote neatly on the bottom of the picture:

Have you seen this man? He was at our school on Monday. If you've seen him, please contact the principal's office.

After Cameron finished writing the flyer, he walked up to Mrs. Nunn's desk.

"Mrs. Nunn, may I go to the office?" he asked.

"For what, Cameron?" Mrs. Nunn said.

"I have to call my mother," Cameron said.

Mrs. Nunn sighed. "Did you leave something at home again?"

"No, not this time," Cameron said. "I just need to ask her something really important. I stay with my mother one week and

then my father the next week. That's why I sometimes forget stuff when I'm going back and forth."

Mrs. Nunn looked surprised. "Why didn't you say something about that before?"

"I don't know," Cameron said softly. "It's been that way since my mother moved back to Austin at the beginning of the school year."

"I see," Mrs. Nunn said. "Cameron, when something changes in your routine at home, I'm here to help you. But I can't help if you don't tell me about it. I can only imagine how hard it is to keep up with things when you're living in two households. Go on and call your mother."

"Thanks, Mrs. Nunn," Cameron said.

Cameron headed for the office to use the phone.

"Mom," Cameron said when she finally answered, "would you do me a favor?"

"Sure, Cameron. What is it?" his mom said.

"I need to have some flyers by lunchtime. Would you make some copies for me?"

"Okay, I'll be right there," his mom said.

"Thanks, Mom," Cameron said. "I'll leave it for you in the office."

"No problem, Cameron. I love you," she said.

Cameron looked around quickly. There were two sixth-grade boys standing next to Ms. Fergins's desk.

"Uh-huh, me, too. 'Bye, Mom," Cameron said as he hung up. He hoped he hadn't hurt his mother's feelings.

"Ms. Fergins," Cameron said. "Do you have an envelope I can put this flyer in? My mom is going to pick it up for me."

"Here you are," Ms. Fergins said as she handed Cameron a large envelope.

"Thank you," Cameron said.

Cameron carefully placed the flyer inside the envelope and sealed it. He wrote his mom's name on the front and gave it to Ms. Fergins. Then he went back to his class.

Cameron and Tarann worked hard to finish their project. Soon, it was lunchtime. Cameron hoped that his mom would bring the flyers on time so that he could pass them out to everyone.

Just then, the loudspeaker crackled.

"Cameron Thompson, please report to the office," Ms. Fergins said.

Mrs. Nunn looked up from the papers she was grading at her desk. "Go on, Cameron," she said.

Cameron almost ran to the office. His mother was waiting for him with a stack of papers.

"Hi, Mom," Cameron said. "Thanks."

She smiled. "Anything for the best artist I know," she said.

"Thanks, Mom," Cameron said, feeling his cheeks flush as Ms. Fergins smiled at him.

"Well, I'll see you after school," his mom said. "Don't forget — tomorrow night you go to your dad's house. I'll miss you."

Cameron wanted to say, "I'll miss you, too, Mom," but a sixth-grade boy leaned on the counter near his elbow and glanced over at them. The words froze in Cameron's throat.

"I'll see you after school," his mom said again. "Good luck with your investigation."

Cameron's mom waved good-bye and walked out of the office. Cameron looked at the boy next to him. He thought about why it mattered so much to him, what this boy's opinion was. He didn't even know him. This boy hadn't gone out of his way to pick up his flyer, make copies, and deliver them. Cameron's mom did that for him, and a lot more. It was time Cameron showed his mom how much he appreciated everything she did for him.

Cameron shouted, "Wait, Mom!"

His mom turned around with a puzzled look on her face.

"What's the matter? Did you forget something, Cameron?" asked his mom.

"Yes," Cameron said, hugging her around the waist. "I forgot to tell you that I love you."

Cameron heard the boy break into laughter.

"Stop that this instant!" Ms. Fergins said sternly.

The laughter stopped immediately.

"Thank you, son," his mom said. "I love you, too. You're turning into a wonderful young man."

A grin popped on Cameron's face. His mom had called him a young man. Maybe she finally realized that he wasn't a baby anymore. He gave her another hug and hurried to the lunchroom to pass out the flyers.

7
Science Fair Surprise

After they had given the flyers to several teachers in the lunchroom, the Mystery-Solving Squad huddled together at a table.

"I still think we shouldn't wait till tomorrow to tell Mr. Garcia about Ken," Tarann said.

"Maybe Tarann is right, Cameron," Jessie said. "Maybe somebody could check his garage and see if the trophy is there."

Cameron said, "We've got bigger fish to fry. I've got a gut feeling about the man in the cowboy hat. My dad says to always trust your gut."

Miguel slapped his stomach. "My gut says I need to eat more and talk less." He opened his lunch bag.

Cameron said, "Got anything for me in there?"

Miguel's mother, Mrs. Oliveras, usually sent an extra dessert for Cameron.

"Sure, she sent your favorite empanadas — apple," Miguel said.

"Tell your mom I said *muchas gracias,*" Cameron said.

"Miguel, maybe you better just tell her that Cameron said *thank you,*" Tarann said. "Cameron's accent is *muy mal.*"

"*Muy mal* means very bad, doesn't it?" Cameron asked. "I don't have a bad accent, do I, Miguel?"

"No, not too bad," Miguel said.

"Hey, there's Mr. Phillips," Jessie said. "We can ask him about the cowboy now."

"I'm really hungry," Cameron said.

"Tarann, will you ask him about the cowboy? And give him a flyer, too."

"Okay," Tarann said. "But save me an empanada, okay?"

"I will," Miguel said.

Tarann grabbed a flyer and took it over to Mr. Phillips. She spoke to him for a few moments and returned to the table.

"Mr. Phillips said he had a couple of cowboys visiting from the rodeo," Tarann said in between bites of her empanada. "But they were young men. He says he remembers the face but doesn't know why. If he's seen the man, he said, it must have been a good while ago."

"Maybe he's related to a student here?" Cameron suggested.

"He would've had to sign in," Miguel said.

"Yeah," Cameron said, "and we've already checked the visitor's book, and no one with an N initial was listed. We also asked Ms. Fergins, and she said she hadn't seen someone with that description."

"Maybe if we show her the picture, it

will help her remember something," Tarann said. "We wanted to hang it in the office anyway."

"That's a great idea," Cameron said. "Let's go."

Tarann and Cameron waited until Ms. Fergins got off the phone. Then they showed her the flyer and explained that this was the cowboy they asked her about earlier.

"Do you recognize this man?" Cameron asked, handing her one of the flyers. "This is a drawing of the cowboy I asked you about earlier. Mr. Phillips says his face looked familiar."

Ms. Fergins stared at the flyer. "Hmmm. He actually looks familiar to me, too, now that I see this picture of him. I can't remember where I've seen him, though. I'll put the flyer up in the office. Maybe one of the other teachers saw this man and can identify him."

"Thank you," Cameron said. "It's really important that we identify him as soon as possible."

"Let's go, Cameron," Tarann said. "We need to get our science project and take it down to the gym for it to be judged."

Cameron and Tarann hurried back to the room and collected everything they needed for their presentation. Mrs. Nunn checked to make sure their project was complete.

"We don't want to forget anything today, now, do we?" Mrs. Nunn said with a smile. "I think you two have an excellent chance of being selected."

"Thanks, Mrs. Nunn," Cameron said.

"Now, hurry," Mrs. Nunn said. "You need to get down to the gym and set everything up before the judging begins."

"Okay," Tarann said. "We're ready. Let's go."

Jessie gave them a thumbs-up from the back of the classroom.

"See you after school," Miguel whispered.

Cameron waved good-bye as he followed Tarann down the hall to the gym.

This was it. If they didn't get chosen to

represent the fourth grade, there would be no chance of having their names engraved on the trophy, even if it was found.

Cameron spotted Kenneth Parker. He was standing with a small group of sixth graders.

"What's Ken doing here?" Tarann asked. "I didn't think he was going to enter the Science Fair."

"He never said he wasn't going to," Cameron said. "It was just that he and Jeff weren't going to be partners."

Mr. Robinson, the sixth-grade science team leader, stood at the microphone.

"Pay attention, fourth graders," Mr. Robinson said. "Before we judge your projects, we've decided to give you a sneak preview of what you'll be up against with our fifth and sixth graders. We have time to show you the top four projects."

The fourth graders watched as the fifth and sixth graders presented their projects. Everyone was impressed. Then the last project was wheeled onto the stage by Kenneth Parker! Cameron and Tarann held their breath.

"Do you think it's the trophy?" Tarann whispered.

Cameron's heart beat so fast it felt like a drumroll in his head.

When Kenneth Parker pulled off the cover, he revealed a tall, colorful rocket ship. It was beautifully designed. Cameron watched Jeff Watson's face. He looked shocked. One thing was clear — the Mystery-Solving Squad was back to square one.

8
The Ring

Cameron and Tarann were the last fourth graders to be judged. They presented their project and the judges seemed pleased. They wouldn't find out who would represent the fourth grade until Friday after school. They went to their lockers and got ready to go home. Miguel and Jessie hurried to catch up with them.

"Well, we're back to the beginning," Cameron said. He explained about Ken's project. "And to make matters worse, we can't even find our only other suspect, the man in the cowboy hat."

"Maybe our flyers will work," Miguel said. "Maybe someone will recognize the man and be able to tell us where to find him."

"Yes, but we only have until tomorrow," Tarann said.

"We're smart enough. Let's put our heads together and think," Jessie said. "Why do you think a cowboy would come to our school?"

"Maybe he went to this school when he was a kid," Cameron said. "Maybe he even won the Science Fair."

"Do you think his ring has something to do with the school?" Jessie said.

"Maybe," Cameron said. "The only person we haven't asked about the cowboy yet is Mr. Garcia. Maybe he'll recognize the cowboy or know about the ring."

When they arrived at the office, Mr. Garcia was sitting behind his desk. His door was wide open. Ms. Fergins was gone for the day.

"Mr. Garcia, could we come in for a minute?" asked Cameron.

Mr. Garcia looked up. "All four of you?"

"Yes, sir," Cameron said. "It won't take long."

"All right," Mr. Garcia said. "But I've got a report to write, so this needs to be quick. What's this about?"

"The missing trophy," Cameron said.

"Have you found it?" Mr. Garcia asked.

"No, sir. Not yet," Cameron said.

"Well, do you have any idea where it might be?" Mr. Garcia asked.

"I think I might know who took the trophy, sir," Cameron said.

"Really?" Mr. Garcia asked. "Who?"

Cameron cleared his throat. He looked at Tarann, Miguel, and Jessie. They looked terrified. "We think the man in the cowboy hat took it, sir," Cameron said.

"What are you talking about? A cowboy? You think a cowboy came to this school and took the Science Fair trophy?" asked Mr. Garcia.

"Yes, we think this man took the trophy," Cameron said, showing Mr. Garcia the flyer. "If we can find this cowboy, Mr. Garcia, we think we'll find the trophy. I . . . I mean, we have a gut feeling about this. I saw this man in front of the trophy case right before it went missing. He said the trophy was going home with him."

Mr. Garcia stared at the flyer.

"Yes, sir," Tarann said quickly. "We agree with Cameron."

Then Miguel spoke up. "We believe Cameron's gut, too, sir. I mean, we agree with Cameron."

"Yes," Jessie finally said. "We think the cowboy took the trophy."

Mr. Garcia looked at each member of the Mystery-Solving Squad and cleared his throat. He rocked back in his chair and looked long and hard at the flyer.

Cameron spoke quickly.

"Mr. Garcia," Cameron said. "I know it's hard to believe that a man wearing a cowboy hat, with a horse on his belt buckle, fancy boots, and a ring with a big N on it, snuck into the school and carried out a huge trophy all by himself."

"That's true," Mr. Garcia said. "But . . ."

"And why would he want it?" Cameron rushed on. "It doesn't make sense. But we believe he took it."

"Well, Cameron," Mr. Garcia said, "the man does look familiar. But I just can't place him right now. And I think I recognize that ring, although I can't recall where. I think you're onto something. See what you can find out and keep me posted. Keep up the good work, kids."

"Thanks, Mr. Garcia," everyone said.

Cameron's mother was waiting for him in the outer office.

"Why weren't you outside?" his mom asked. "I looked all over for you."

"I'm sorry, Mom," Cameron said. "We were working on our case. Honest."

"Okay, but we need to go now," his mother said. "You can talk about your case later on the phone. Come on, kids. I'll give you all rides home."

As they walked out, Jessie said, "Your mom's cool."

"Yes, she is," Cameron said.

Cameron's mom dropped off Tarann, Miguel, and Jessie at their homes. When they pulled into their own driveway, his mom said, "Cameron, I showed your drawing to some people at my real estate office. And guess what — they didn't recognize the cowboy, but they *did* recognize the ring he's wearing."

Cameron sat up. "What did they tell you?" he asked.

"One of my coworkers told me that the ring is worn by a group of scientists here in Austin," she said. "They call themselves the Newton Club, after Sir Isaac Newton, the famous scientist from the sixteen hundreds. Each member wears that gold ring with an N on it. The group started here at Pecan Springs Elementary. Maybe you can find out something about it in the school library."

"Mom," Cameron said, "you're the coolest. Thanks for everything! Maybe this is the clue we need to solve the case."

After dinner, Cameron and the Mystery-Solving Squad had another conference call. Cameron told them what his mom had said about the ring. Then he asked them to meet him at school a little early the next day so they could research the Newton Club in the library.

That night, Cameron could barely sleep. He was excited and anxious at the same time. Tomorrow afternoon he would know whether he and Tarann were chosen to compete in the district-wide Science Fair. And tomorrow he'd finally have the chance to find out who the cowboy is and maybe even locate the missing trophy.

9
Crime Scene Clues

The Mystery-Solving Squad was waiting for Cameron when he got to school. "Let's go straight to the library," Cameron said.

Lining the school's library wall were historic photographs about the school from the day it opened in 1940. Cameron had never really looked that closely at the pictures before. But he knew that if the Newton Club had started their club at the school, their picture would be on the wall.

"Jessie, you and Miguel start over there and look at that wall of photographs,"

Cameron said, "and Tarann and I will check out the ones on this wall. We'll meet in the center."

Cameron looked carefully at each photograph. Sometimes people didn't look anything like their pictures. None of the men were dressed like cowboys. They all had on dark blue or black suits. Suddenly, Cameron stopped in front of a large, gold-framed photograph. There was a photo of the cowboy! His name was Felix Evans III. Underneath his name was a label that read, *Scientist, Philanthropist, and Founding Member of the Newton Club.*

"Hey, everyone! Come over here," Cameron said. "Here he is! You can even see his ring. It's got that big N in the center. And it says he's a founding member of the Newton Club. That's the group my mom told me about."

"So, now we finally know his name," Tarann said. "Felix Evans III."

"Now we can tell Mr. Garcia," Jessie said.

"We need to hurry up," said Tarann. "The

morning bell will ring soon. I don't want to be late for class."

The Mystery-Solving Squad hurried to their classroom. They had barely sat down in class before Cameron heard their names called over the intercom. "Cameron Thompson, Miguel Oliveras, Jessie Rivas, and Tarann Johnson, please come to the office."

Mrs. Nunn said, "Go ahead."

The Mystery-Solving Squad hurried to the principal's office.

When they got there, Cameron saw his dad, Detective Richard Thompson, talking with Mr. Garcia.

"Hi, Dad," Cameron said. "What are you doing here?"

"Hi, son. Hi, kids," Detective Thompson said. "Your mother told me you were working on a big case. I came by to see if I could help."

Cameron explained everything that had happened on the case. Then he showed his father the flyer he had posted in the office.

"We found out this morning that his name is Felix Evans III," Cameron said. "His ring is the symbol for the Newton Club. He's the founder."

"Now I remember," Mr. Garcia said. "Mr. Evans's family donated the case where the Science Fair trophy was displayed."

"Let's go down to the scene of the crime," Detective Thompson said. They all walked down to the display case.

"Look," Cameron said, pointing to the plaque above the display case. "It says, *Donated by the Evans Family, 1965.*"

"If he donated the display case, maybe he has one of the keys," Miguel said.

"That's possible," Detective Thompson said.

"We think Mr. Evans took the trophy out of the case and then used Mr. Murray's dolly to take it down the hall and out the back door," Cameron said.

"We found black tread marks in front of the trophy case," Tarann explained.

"Mr. Garcia, I think the kids are onto

something," Detective Thompson said. "Do you know how we can get in touch with Mr. Evans?"

"Yes, I have his contact information," Mr. Garcia said. "He's always been a big supporter of Pecan Springs and the Science Fair. But he's been in poor health over the last few years and hasn't visited the school for a while. That's why I couldn't remember where I'd seen the face on your flyer."

"Do you think he'd take the trophy?" Detective Thompson asked.

"No, I'm sure Mr. Evans wouldn't steal anything," Mr. Garcia said. "He's a millionaire — he could buy all the trophies in Austin! Why would he sneak into an elementary school and steal ours?"

"Well, the only way to find out is to ask him," Detective Thompson said. "Let's pay him a visit."

"I'll go with you," Mr. Garcia said.

"Can we go, Dad?" Cameron asked. "It's our case. You always say a detective should stick with his case."

"Son," said Detective Thompson, "it's up to Mr. Garcia. I don't mind, but Mr. Garcia is the principal and you're at school."

Mr. Garcia turned to Miguel, Jessie, and Tarann. "If you can get permission from your parents while I look up Mr. Evans's address, you can go," Mr. Garcia said as he went into his office.

Miguel, Jessie, and Tarann rushed to the phone to call their parents.

"You must be tired, son," Detective Thompson said with a smile. "All this detective work, keeping up with your school assignments, and entering the Science Fair! You've done a great job on this case. I'm proud of you."

"Thanks, Dad," Cameron said. "I learned everything about being a detective from you. And Mom's been a big help, too. I just hope we can solve this case today."

10
A Visit With Mr. Evans

Miguel, Tarann, and Jessie all got permission from their parents. They rushed over to tell Detective Thompson that they could go with him.

"The Mystery-Solving Squad is about to close this case," Jessie said.

"I hope so," Tarann said.

"Me, too," Miguel said.

"Okay, everyone," Mr. Garcia said. "I have his address. He's at the Gardenville Assisted-Living Home. It's just a few blocks away from the school."

"Let's go," Detective Thompson said.

When they arrived at the Gardenville Assisted-Living Home, they immediately went to the office. The home didn't look the way Cameron had pictured it. He looked around. He saw women in one room doing exercises. He could hear laughter and music off in the distance.

The director of the home, Dr. Larry Dixon, greeted them and shook everyone's hand. "What can I do for you today?" he asked.

"The elementary school is missing its Science Fair trophy, Dr. Dixon," said Detective Thompson, "and we have reason to believe that Mr. Evans may have had something to do with it."

Cameron pulled out his flyer and handed it to Dr. Dixon. "I saw Mr. Evans in the hallway at school on the day the trophy was taken. He said the trophy was going home with him," said Cameron.

Dr. Dixon looked impressed. "You can draw very well, son. It's amazing how you captured his look." Cameron smiled.

"Can we speak to him? We're not saying he took the trophy, but he might be able to help us find it," said Detective Thompson.

"When he's feeling well and wants a little adventure, Mr. Evans sometimes slips away. Believe me, one minute he's here and the next minute he's gone."

Dr. Dixon was right! Cameron remembered how quietly the cowboy had snuck up on him and then how he'd just sort of disappeared.

"He wasn't feeling well on Monday evening. But I understand he's feeling better today. Let's go up to his apartment," Dr. Dixon said. "He's got an entire suite on the top floor. He has a nurse, but he can't keep up with him."

Detective Thompson glanced at Mr. Garcia, who looked surprised. When Dr. Dixon rang the doorbell, a man in a white uniform opened the door. "Hello, can I help you, Dr. Dixon?"

"Mr. Farley, it seems that a trophy is

missing from Pecan Springs Elementary School. Has Mr. Evans brought in anything like that lately?" asked Dr. Dixon.

"Not that I know of," Mr. Farley said. "But he called a cab and slipped away on Monday while I was running some errands for him. I don't know where he went, but it tired him out."

"We'd just like to talk to him," Detective Thompson said.

"Come with me. He's in the den," Mr. Farley said.

He led them into a book-lined room with a fireplace and several comfortable chairs.

"Mr. Evans, we have guests," Mr. Farley said.

An older man dressed in a crisp white shirt, blue jeans, and cowboy boots rose to greet them.

"There's the belt buckle," Jessie whispered to Cameron.

Mr. Evans was wearing the belt with the horse on the buckle.

"My goodness," Mr. Evans said, "who are these young scholars?" He thrust his hand toward Cameron.

"I'm Cameron Thompson, sir," Cameron said, sticking out his hand. "And this is Tarann Johnson, Miguel Oliveras, Jessie Rivas, our principal, Mr. Garcia, and my father, Detective Thompson."

"Would you all like to sit down?" Mr. Evans asked. "I haven't had my midday tea. We could all have tea together."

"Thank you, sir," Mr. Garcia said. "That would be nice."

"I'll get the tea," Mr. Farley said.

Mr. Evans said, "I don't like drinking tea alone. I don't like being alone."

Cameron felt sad for Mr. Evans. He wouldn't like being alone, either.

Mr. Farley returned with a tray of cookies, punch, a pot of tea, and several teacups. He served everyone and then left the room.

"Now, how can I help you?" Mr. Evans asked.

There was a long silence. Finally, Cameron glanced at Mr. Garcia, who nodded his head.

"Mr. Evans, I don't know if you remember me, but we met in the hallway in front of the trophy case at Pecan Springs on Monday," Cameron said.

"Ah, yes," Mr. Evans said. "You were examining the trophy with your magnifying glass."

"Yes, sir," Cameron said. "You told me you were going to take the trophy home with you."

Mr. Evans put his teacup down with a crash. He looked stunned.

"Oh, my!" Mr. Evans said. "I am so very sorry. I took the trophy out of the case on Monday to have it polished. I was going to surprise the school. I left a note on Mr. Garcia's desk," Mr. Evans said.

"I've been working on a stack of reports all week," Mr. Garcia said. "Your note probably got buried underneath my work."

"But, Mr. Evans, how did you open the trophy case?" Detective Thompson asked.

"Well, as you may know, my family donated the display case to the school. I've always had a key," Mr. Evans said. A big smile broke out on Miguel's face. He had guessed right about how Mr. Evans got into the trophy case! Mr. Evans continued, "So I just unlocked the case and removed the trophy. I noticed a blue case on the floor, so I put it where the trophy had stood, for safekeeping. I used the dolly I found on the loading dock to move the trophy to the cab. Then I dropped the trophy off at a repair shop not far from here."

"So that's how my magnifying-glass case got inside the display case!" Cameron said.

"I'm sorry," Mr. Evans said. "I wasn't feeling well on Monday night and for the next few days. I completely forgot that I left the trophy at the trophy shop to be polished. I'm so sorry if I've caused you or the school any trouble."

Mr. Garcia cleared his throat. "Don't worry about it, sir. I was the one who buried your note, after all! I think we've bothered you enough for one day. Thank you for everything you've done to support Pecan Springs Elementary School."

"I like to do what I can," Mr. Evans said. "One of my favorite things to do is volunteer and help students, especially at Pecan Springs."

Cameron realized that he really liked Mr. Evans. He didn't seem as scary as he had in the hall that day.

"Mr. Evans," Cameron said. "Tarann and I entered a project in the Science Fair. We find out this afternoon if we're going to be in the district-wide competition. Do you want to come to the assembly this afternoon? I mean, since you're a scientist yourself."

"Why, thank you for that kind invitation," Mr. Evans said with a smile. "I'd love to attend."

"I can come pick you up if you'd like," Detective Thompson offered.

"Thank you," Mr. Evans said. "I'd appreciate that."

"Thank you for everything, Mr. Evans,"

Cameron said as they all got up to leave. "I'll see you this afternoon."

"See you then," Mr. Evans said with a smile. "And do come back and have tea with me again soon. I really enjoyed talking with all of you."

"We will," Jessie promised.

"You can count on it," Miguel said.

As they drove back to school, Detective Thompson said, "Well, I think the case of the missing trophy is officially closed. Good work, kids."

"I think the Mystery-Solving Squad should restart the Pecan Springs chapter of the Newton Club," Tarann said. "We're all interested in science."

"That's a great idea," Jessie said.

"Maybe we can ask Mr. Evans if he'd like to be one of our sponsors," Cameron said.

"I bet he'd enjoy that," Miguel said. "And he can tell us about the original projects the Newton Club did when he was at Pecan Springs."

"Well, here we are," Detective Thompson

said as they drove up in front of the school. "I'm going back to my office."

"Thanks for your help, Detective Thompson," Mr. Garcia said. "It's good to know I have two detectives named Thompson that I can call on in times of need."

"And now there's the whole Mystery-Solving Squad at Pecan Springs," Jessie said.

Everyone laughed.

"Mr. Evans and I will be back this afternoon for the Science Fair assembly," Detective Thompson said. "See you all soon."

"Good-bye, Dad," Cameron said.

"Come into my office," Mr. Garcia said to the Mystery-Solving Squad. "Let's see if we can find the note Mr. Evans said he left for me when he took the trophy."

Everyone carefully searched Mr. Garcia's desk for the note.

"Here it is!" Tarann said, picking up a piece of paper from under the chair in front of Mr. Garcia's desk.

"Well, if my desk were a little neater, the

case of the missing trophy would never have happened," Mr. Garcia said.

"But then we wouldn't have had a chance to meet Mr. Evans," Cameron said.

"That made all our detective work worthwhile," Tarann said.

"That's a good way to look at it," Mr. Garcia said. "Now, I'll write a pass for all of you so you can get back to class. Thanks again for your hard work."

"You're welcome, Mr. Garcia," Cameron said. "It was hard, but we had fun!"

The Mystery-Solving Squad went back to class. The rest of the afternoon flew by, and soon the last bell rang. It was time to go to the lunchroom for the Science Fair assembly. Tarann and Cameron sat with the other applicants. Miguel and Jessie found seats near the back of the room.

"I'm really nervous," Tarann said.

"Don't worry. We have a great project," Cameron said. "And we did our best work. I'm sure we'll be picked."

"I hope so," Tarann said. "I really hope so."

"Here comes my dad with Mr. Evans," Cameron said. He waved at his father. Detective Thompson and Mr. Evans waved back.

"Good to see you both again," Mr. Evans said. "Are you excited?"

"Very," Cameron said.

"Well, best of luck to both of you," Mr. Evans said. "If you're smart enough to track down the missing trophy, I know you'll do well in the science competition."

"Thank you, Mr. Evans," Tarann said.

"We'd better sit down," Detective Thompson said. "The judges are getting ready to make the announcement."

Cameron held his breath as Mr. Robinson, one of the Science Fair judges, walked to the microphone.

"Thank you for entering your projects in the Science Fair," Mr. Robinson said. "We enjoyed reviewing your experiments. It's unfortunate that only two projects per grade can be entered in the district-wide contest. And now for the winners! Our sixth-grade representatives are Anysa Bailey and Kenneth Parker. Anysa and Ken, please come up to the front."

Cameron and Tarann exchanged looks. Then they looked over at Jeff Watson. He seemed stunned that his project wasn't picked and that Ken was chosen as a sixth-grade representative.

"That just goes to show that it never pays to mistreat anyone," Tarann said. "Jeff probably didn't think Ken would create a winning project without his help."

"Well, he was wrong," Cameron said.

Mr. Robinson continued. "Our fifth-grade representatives are Allison Derrett and Micah Eargle. Please come forward," he said.

"I'm so nervous!" Tarann said.

"And now for our fourth-grade representatives," Mr. Robinson said. "David Oshoko and the team of Tarann Johnson and Cameron Thompson. Please come forward. Congratulations, everyone!"

Tarann and Cameron high-fived each other and rushed to the front of the lunch-room to stand next to the other finalists. Cameron looked for his dad and Mr. Evans. He didn't see them anywhere.

"Where are my dad and Mr. Evans?" Cameron whispered to Tarann. They looked around the room but couldn't find them.

"Maybe Mr. Evans didn't feel well, and your dad had to take him home," Tarann said. Cameron felt disappointed. Miguel and Jessie gave him a thumbs-up. He tried to smile.

"That concludes the announcements," Mr. Robinson said. "However, we have two special guests who would like to speak to you."

The curtains on the stage opened. Detective Thompson and Mr. Evans stood on either side of the Science Fair trophy. It had been cleaned and polished. It glowed under the lights. It looked brand-new!

"Ooohh," everyone said.

Mr. Robinson handed the microphone to Mr. Evans.

"For those of you who may not know me, my name is Felix Evans," he said. "It is my great pleasure to return the Science Fair trophy back to the display case. I want to congratulate all of the representatives from Pecan Springs Elementary School."

Mr. Evans looked directly at Cameron and Tarann. Then he continued, "And I feel confident that this trophy will return to the display case at Pecan Springs after the district-wide Science Fair next month." Everyone applauded and Mr. Evans bowed slightly.

Mr. Robinson dismissed everyone back to their classrooms. But he asked Cameron, Tarann, Miguel, and Jessie to stay behind. "Mr. Evans has a special request for you," Mr. Robinson told the Mystery-Solving Squad.

Mr. Evans led the group to the display case. "I think that there are a few special students who should place the trophy back inside the case," Mr. Evans said. "Cameron,

Tarann, Miguel, and Jessie, please give me a hand."

The Mystery-Solving Squad helped Mr. Evans lift the trophy into the case. It sparkled like a golden jewel under the display lights.

"Well, another case closed," Cameron said.

"All for one," Jessie said.

"And one for all," they said together.